Knitty kitty

DAVID ELLIOTT

illustrated by CHRISTOPHER DENISE

CANDLEWICK PRESS

Clickety-click.
Tickety-tick.
Knitty Kitty sits and knits.

"A hat for me, Knitty Kitty?"

"Yes, little kitten. A hat. To keep you cozy."

Tickety-tick.
Clickety-click.
Knitty Kitty sits and knits.

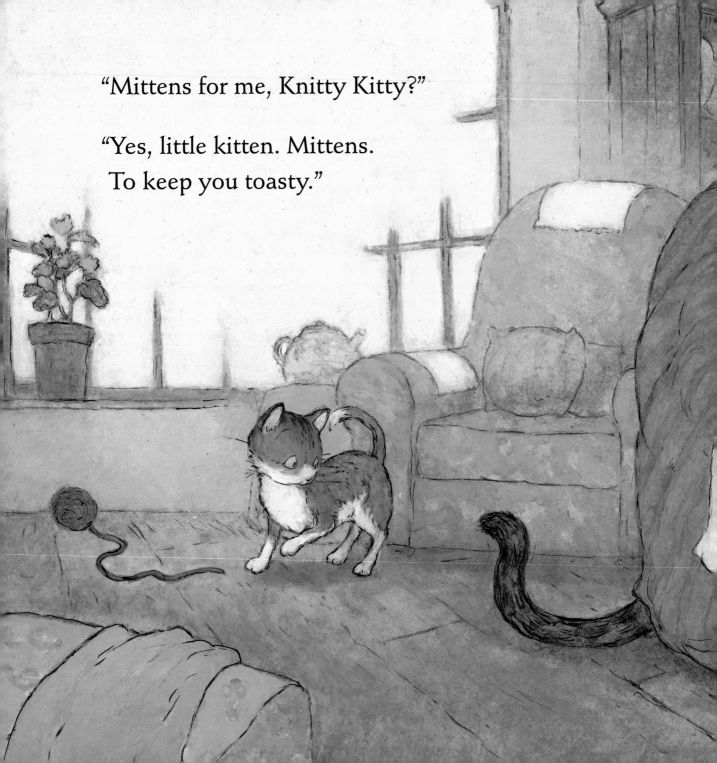

"Mittens for me, Knitty Kitty?"

"Yes, little kitten. Mittens.
To keep you toasty."

Clickety-click.
Lickety-split.
Knitty Kitty sits and knits.

"A hat for me, Knitty Kitty?
Mittens for me?"

"No, little kitten. A scarf. To keep you comfy."

But snowmen like to be cozy, too.
At least, that's what kittens think.

The winter moon rises.
Knitty Kitty rings her bell.

It's bedtime for kittens everywhere.

"Come along, little kittens."

But the kittens can't sleep.
"We're not cozy!" they meow. "We're not comfy. We're not toasty!"

"Don't worry," purrs Knitty Kitty.
"I have something to keep you warm."

"What is it, Knitty Kitty?" the kittens cry.

"Me!"

"Cozy!"

"Night-night, little kittens."

"Night-night, Knitty Kitty."

"Night-night."

"Night-night."

"Night-night."